Ashleigh Lewis

SPIKE
The Tramp

Home Farm Twins

Spike
The Tramp

Jenny Oldfield

Illustrated by Kate Aldous

Hodder
Children's
Books

a division of Hodder Headline plc

First published in Great Britain in 1996
by Hodder Children's Books
a division of Hodder Headline plc
338 Euston Road
London NW1 3BH

10 9 8 7 6 5 4 3 2 1

A Catalogue record for this book is available from the British Library

ISBN 0 340 66131 3

Typeset by Avon Dataset Ltd, Bidford-on-Avon, Warks

Printed and bound in Great Britain by
Cox & Wyman Ltd, Reading, Berks

One

'Piglet!' Hannah cried.

David Moore looked up sharply from his magazine. 'Hannah, don't be rude to your twin sister!'

Hannah and Helen looked across the kitchen table at one another and giggled.

'No, Dad, she's not talking to me,' Helen spoke between mouthfuls of cake. 'She's reading a book about hedgehogs.'

'Yes, and it says here that the babies are called piglets. Isn't that sweet?' Hannah showed them a picture of five spiky balls curled up in a leafy nest beside a mother hedgehog. 'They eat slugs and insects, and worms and grubs.'

'Do you mind?' Helen swallowed her last portion of cake. 'Not while I'm eating!'

'Yum-yum, worms!' David Moore teased to get his own back. 'Creepy-crawlies, crunchy beetles . . .' He smacked his lips and made snorting, snuffling sounds.

'Did you know, hedgehogs can run at five miles an hour?' Hannah read out. 'Some of them travel up to two miles a night. Wow!'

'Vroom-vroom!' Their dad pretended to drive a racing car. 'Formula One hedgehogs!'

'Da-ad!' the twins protested.

'I'm writing a hedgehog project for school,' Hannah told him. 'I'm serious.'

'Take no notice,' their mum said, coming into the kitchen. She was wrapped up ready to take their dog, Speckle, for a walk. It was six o'clock on a cold November evening, and already dark outside. 'Does anyone fancy coming with us?'

'Me!'

'Me!' The twins scrambled to the door.

'Not me!' David Moore was happy to stay in the cosy farmhouse kitchen.

Speckle barked and jumped for his lead. Mary took it down from the hook.

'We can go hedgehog-spotting,' Helen suggested. She preferred action to reading a book. 'They come out at night, so we should see some if we look hard.'

'If they've any sense they'll already be curled up nice and warm for the winter.' Their dad snuggled by the fire in his chunky sweater. His feet toasted inside his slippers, his wavy hair was ruffled.

'Not yet, but soon.' Hannah was sure of her hedgehog facts. 'They're still busy building nests and stocking up on food.'

'Watch out, slugs!' he called, as they opened the door on to a dark farmyard, and Helen, Hannah, Mary and Speckle vanished into the windy night.

'There's one!' Helen shone her torch on the ground as she crawled along. The hedge-bottom smelt of damp leaves. 'Here, Hannah, quick!' The hedgehog heard her and turned.

Hannah had brought their dad's camera out on the dog walk. Frosty air nipped their ears, fingers and toes. Old cobwebs hung in the hedge like white lace. They were in the lane heading down from Home Farm to Doveton village, by the gate to Crackpot Farm. Sam Lawson, a boy in their class, lived there with his mum and dad.

'Quick, Hannah, he's spotted me!'

Hannah ran to the gate, climbed over it and crawled into the ditch beside Helen. As she pointed the camera at a scuffling ball of spines, legs and little black snout, Speckle too came bounding across.

'Here boy!' Mrs Moore called him back in vain.

Click! Hannah pressed the camera shutter. *Click, click, whirr*! There was a flash of white light, and a second when Speckle pushed his wet nose at the spiky little creature. He yelped and bounced back. Then the hedgehog rolled into a tight ball.

'Aah, poor Speckle!' Helen couldn't help laughing. The young sheepdog hung his head as he trotted slowly back to their mum with his prickled nose.

'I got it,' Hannah said, proudly holding up the camera. 'I can put this picture in my project.'

'Good for you.' Mary Moore stamped her feet in the cold lane. 'I'll take Speckle on ahead and leave you to your hedgehog studies. But don't be long. I'll see you back home in ten minutes.'

The twins promised, but they found it hard to take

their eyes off the hedgehog. 'How long will he stay rolled up in a ball?' Helen whispered. Her breath blew clouds of steam into the air.

'Until he thinks he's safe.' Hannah backed off. The hedgehog was tiny; probably a young one, not much more than a piglet. 'Shh!' She dragged Helen back with her.

Together they squatted in Crackpot Farm gateway, waiting for him to unroll.

At last, thinking all was clear, the hedgehog flattened his spines and poked out his nose. It was long, pointed and wet. His eyes were bright and black. A furry face, long whiskers and a mass of sharp speckled spines completed the picture.

'Look at his sweet face. It's almost white!' Hannah whispered. 'Most of them are brown.' She watched him shuffle here and there, snouting for food. 'Fetch him a slug!' she told Helen.

'You fetch him a slug!' Helen shuddered.

So Hannah poked in the dark ditch. 'Slugs are off,' she reported back. 'How about a nice juicy beetle?' She shone her torch under a bramble, spotted a crunchy black insect lying, legs in the air. Swiftly she picked it up between her finger and thumb.

Helen screwed up her mouth and stared.

'It's OK, it's dead.' She dangled it in front of the hedgehog. 'Here, boy!'

'Stop it, he isn't a dog.'

'Just you watch.' Hannah's eyes glistened in the moonlight.

Sniff-sniff-snort-snuffle! He picked up the scent of the beetle, forgot his fear and trotted towards the treat.

'The way to a hedgehog's heart is through his stomach,' Hannah announced. 'It says so in the book.' She dropped the beetle under his nose.

Snap, crackle, pop! It was gone.

Helen pulled another face. She curled her mouth in disgust.

'That's lip-smackingly gorgeous for a hedgehog. Fast food. Now, what's for pudding?' Hannah began to poke around in the ditch again.

'Come on, let's go.' Helen pulled her away. She'd had enough wildlife study for one night. 'You got your photo, didn't you?'

'OK.' Reluctantly Hannah agreed. But as they climbed the gate back into the lane, the greedy hedgehog followed. He trundled under the bottom bar, snuffling as he came. 'Oh look, he's still hungry!' Hannah turned to see him trotting up to them, nose twitching. 'Isn't he cute?'

'Hmm.' Helen hadn't forgotten the beetle. But then she saw the trail of little footprints through the frosty grass, and his shiny, twitching nose. Overhead a barn owl hooted. 'I suppose,' she admitted.

Hannah put her hand in her pocket. She'd brought her piece of cake with her, wrapped in a serviette. Now she took it out and sprinkled a few crumbs in the lane. The hedgehog was on to them in a flash. He seemed to suck them clear off the ground.

'Let's take him home,' Hannah joked. 'We need a new Hoover!'

So they laid a trail of crumbs, and sure enough, the hedgehog followed.

Helen and Hannah grinned to see him trundle up their lane behind them. 'We could show Dad,' Helen suggested. Their father was a wildlife photographer, working right now on animals that only came out at night. He took fantastic pictures of owls, foxes, badgers and little hedgehogs like this one.

'If only we could get him to come and stay at Home Farm,' Hannah sighed.

'Who, Dad?' Helen frowned.

'No, stupid. Spike!'

'Spike who?'

'This Spike!' She pointed to the willing hedgehog, still hoovering up the crumbs.

'Oh, so he's Spike now?' Helen considered the name. 'I didn't know we were on first-name terms. Next I suppose you'll want to adopt him?'

The twins had already brought hens, rabbits, a goose, a dog and a pony to Home Farm since they arrived earlier that year. Helen wasn't so keen on hedgehogs, she decided.

'You bet!' Hannah's face shone in the torchlight. 'We can look after him and feed him until it's time for him to hibernate.' Every animal was welcome at Home Farm as far as she was concerned. 'Then he can stay in our barn all winter!'

'That'll be fun!' Helen preferred her animals to do cleverer things, like Solo their pony, or Speckle their dog. As far as she could see, a hibernating hedgehog was about as exciting as watching paint dry.

'Yes!' Hannah trailed more crumbs up the lane. Spike gobbled, trotted, and gobbled his way towards Home Farm. 'He can't actually be a pet, because hedgehogs hate being put in cages. They love freedom.'

'Hmm.' Helen studied him.

'They come and go, just minding their own business.'

She liked the sound of this better.

Hannah backed round a corner and laid the trail of crumbs into their own farm. It was all quiet in the frosty night, except for dead leaves rustling across the yard. She peered at her sister from under her woolly hat. 'They rummage and root around for food, then they move on.'

'Like a tramp,' Helen said softly. She got down on her hands and knees, to hedgehog-level. Spike munched his way towards the barn.

'Yes, like a tramp,' agreed Hannah.

The twins crouched and watched as Spike sniffed the new scents: flaking paint and old wood of the barn door, straw in Solo's stall, earwigs, insects and slugs!

He grunted. Sharp claws scuffled amongst dead weeds. The last the twins saw of Spike before their mum called them into the house, he was scurrying under the barn door, his mouth full of leaves and straw.

Two

'Spike's building a nest.'

'For his first winter.'

'He's staying with us.'

'We saw him.'

Hannah and Helen gave the good news over breakfast next morning. They'd already been out to the barn and discovered his winter home. It was a pile of twigs and leaves under a rusty iron plough. They'd watched him finish making the pile, which he'd gathered overnight, and this morning, as dawn broke, he'd turned it into a hedgehog nest.

'He dives into the middle of the heap!' Helen

dropped her spoon into her cereal bowl. She jumped
up to show her mum and dad how Spike had done it.
'Then he turns round and round on the spot like this.'
Since watching his performance, she'd changed her
mind about hedgehogs. 'He's brilliant!'

'He uses his spikes to comb the leaves into a big
round ball, with him inside,' Hannah continued.

'Then he just curls up and goes to sleep,' said
Helen.

'Lucky hedgehog,' David Moore sighed. Soon he
had to go out and face the cold morning. Saturday was
his day for driving into Nesfield with their mum to
shop.

'It's your dad's dream,' Mary Moore smiled, 'to
snooze away the winter.' She was ready to set off
bright and early. Though she'd closed her health food
café in Nesfield until spring, she was still busy there.
Today she was going to clean all the paintwork,
scrubbing it until it gleamed. The car was stacked
with soap and scrubbing-brushes, mops, buckets and
cloths.

'Come and look,' Hannah invited her dad. She
wanted him to inspect Spike's new nest before they
set off. 'No, not you, Speckle. You'd better stay here.

Dogs and hedgehogs don't mix.'

'You're sure we won't disturb him?' David Moore followed the twins to the barn. It was a clear, sharp morning. The sky was bright blue, and every distant tree on Doveton Fell was picked out by the winter sunlight.

Helen eased open the wide door. It creaked and groaned. Inside his stall, Solo tossed his head at them and softly whinnied. 'No, it's OK. Come in,' she replied.

Out of the wind the barn was warm and shadowy. They tiptoed to the rusty plough, holding their breaths. A cobweb brushed Hannah's face, and David Moore stumbled against a stack of old garden tools hidden in the straw.

'Ugh!'

'Ouch!'

'Shh!' Helen put her finger to her lip. She bent to look under the plough. But instead of the neat ball hiding a sleeping Spike, there was only a messy heap of scattered leaves. She stared, then turned to Hannah. 'He's not here!'

Hannah saw for herself. 'Where is he?'

The twins were shocked and upset. Their new lodger had vanished.

'I expect he decided to move on.' Their dad took a quick look round.

'But the barn's perfect!' For a moment Helen felt cross. Apparently Spike hadn't appreciated their offer of a place to stay.

'Yes, but hedgehogs have minds of their own.' David Moore went out into the fresh air, checking the yard for any signs of Spike. He looked under the stone trough beside the kitchen door, then behind the wooden rabbit hutch under the chestnut tree. 'Sorry, girls, it looks as if he's gone walkabout.'

Hannah sniffed. 'Never mind.' She tried to hide her disappointment. 'I expect he's gone after some tasty slugs. He can't be ready to hibernate yet.'

'Tramps don't like roofs over their heads, do they?' Helen worked it out; perhaps Spike had felt hemmed-in inside the barn. Maybe Home Farm was too crowded for him, with Solo in his stall, Speckle bounding about in the yard, Sugar and Spice, the rabbits, snug in their hutch, the chickens pecking in the dirt, Lucy the goose in her field . . .

Both twins nodded and sighed. 'Ah, well.' Hannah still had her school project to work on, and her photograph of Spike from last night to remember him by.

They stood on the bottom bar of the gate, elbows resting along the top as it swung gently to and fro; two dark-haired girls with big brown eyes, alike as two peas. After they'd driven into town on the dreaded shopping trip, they would be back home with a whole weekend ahead of them.

Then they would saddle up Solo and ride, one on the pony, one on a bike, down into Doveton to see friends. Speckle would come with them. They would see the lake sparkle in the sun, visit John Fox and Ben at Lakeside Farm, call in on Luke Martin and his white doves at the village shop. There were animals everywhere: sheep on the fell, dogs on the farms, Sultan the thoroughbred at Doveton Manor.

'Oh well,' Helen said again as she climbed into the car. Life wasn't so bad.

They drove down the lane past Crackpot Farm and High Hartwell. Hannah stared out at the bare hedges and mossy walls. 'But I wonder where Spike is now?' she sighed.

On the move, tramping through ditches, making another nest. He was living the open air life.

'Hi, Laura!' Helen waved at their friend, Laura

Saunders. It was Saturday afternoon, and she'd ridden Solo down to his old home of Doveton Manor to see Laura's new horse. Hannah had freewheeled down the hill on her bike, while Speckle loped after them.

Laura glanced over the paddock fence and smiled. She was working hard, lunging her magnificent black horse. But she stopped to talk. 'Hi, you two.' She patted the grey pony's neck. 'What are you up to?'

'Nothing much.' Hannah scanned the green lawn beside the manor house, peering closely at the shrubs and bushes.

'Yes you are,' Laura said. 'You're looking for something.'

'No-o!' Helen denied it. In fact, they'd been searching hard all the way down the hill.

'Or someone?' Laura knew they were animal crazy. 'It doesn't have four legs by any chance?'

'Well, as a matter of fact . . .' Hannah was about to confess.

'It's a little hedgehog,' Helen admitted. 'This big.' She held her hands about twenty centimetres apart. 'He's quite fat at the moment, because we fed him lots of cake . . .'

Laura began to laugh. 'Does he know you're looking for him?'

Hannah blushed. 'We just want to check he's OK. He's quite young, you see, and all on his own. We're worried he might not build a proper nest in time for winter.'

'Don't hedgehogs know how to look after themselves?' Laura held Sultan on a short rein. The two horses nudged each other, while Speckle scampered across the paddock.

'Yes, we're not *really* worried,' Helen put in. 'Anyway, I don't suppose we'll ever know.' They'd looked for tracks in the mud, even stopped to search in the hedge at the gateway to Crackpot Farm. There was no sign of Spike going back the way he'd come.

They chatted with Laura, then called Speckle and moved on towards Doveton Main Street, with its neat slate cottages and long gardens. Mr Winter's dog, Puppy, barked at his front gate. The old schoolteacher came out of the house and frowned at them.

But Luke Martin had a smile on his face when Hannah went into the shop for crisps. 'Hello, Helen. What can I do for you?'

'I'm Hannah,' she said absent-mindedly. 'Luke, do

you know anything about hedgehogs?'

The shopkeeper didn't seem to consider it a strange question. 'Let's see, little round things with sharp spikes. Get into lots of car accidents, worse luck.'

Hannah shuddered. 'Don't!' This was her main worry about Spike. Did he know the dangers of the road as he set off on his wanderings? She explained how they'd hoped to give Spike a safe place to stay after they'd first found him by the gate at Crackpot Farm.

Luke listened quietly. 'Well, when he's ready he'll settle down, no doubt. Hang on a sec.' He turned towards a back room behind the shop. 'Sam!'

A boy with hair the colour of straw and a round, rosy face appeared. It was Luke's nephew, Sam Lawson, from Crackpot Farm. He went to Doveton Junior School with the twins, but they didn't know him well.

'How are you on recognising hedgehogs? Can you tell one from another?' his uncle asked.

Sam frowned. 'They all look the same to me.'

'About this long. He's only young, with a very pale face. That's how you'd know him.' Hannah felt her own face burning with embarrassment. 'He's much paler than most hedgehogs; nearly white really.' She'd left Helen waiting with Solo and Speckle outside the shop. The way Sam Lawson was staring at her, she wished she'd never come in. Or she wished she could get hedgehogs out of her mind. People were beginning to look at her strangely.

'You'll keep a lookout, won't you, Sam? Helen says they found the little chap in the hedge by your place.'

'Hannah,' she said faintly.

'That's right, Hannah. Let them know at Home Farm if you spot him. They wanted to adopt him for the winter, but he wasn't having any.'

Sam stared even harder. 'OK,' he said slowly. Then he disappeared into the back room.

'He must like you,' Like teased as she bought her crisps. 'He's normally very shy, but you actually managed to get a word out of him.'

It went on all afternoon; the twins stopping to talk while Speckle nosed about happily and Solo stood patiently waiting. With everyone they met it was the same thing. Helen would mention the weather, school and *hedgehogs*. Hannah peered into gardens, yards, ditches and hedges, looking for *hedgehogs*. When Speckle ran ahead to Lakeside Farm, nose to the ground, they followed. When he stopped short at the ancient farmhouse and began to snuffle at a pile of logs by the door, their hearts missed a beat.

'Speckle?' By now it was Hannah's turn to ride Solo. She jumped down from the saddle and led the pony across the yard.

'What have you found?' Helen dropped the bike and ran to the logs.

Speckle darted at the pile, braked, put his head to one side and barked. He glanced up at the twins with a puzzled look: *I don't know what this is exactly, but it's the same thing that gave me a jab on the nose last night. I'm not going anywhere near it*! He stood at a safe distance.

'Spike?' Helen and Hannah cried together. The hedgehog was the right size, but was it him? He was rolled tight, his telltale face hidden from sight. As the farm door opened and John Fox peered out, Helen fell to her knees for a closer look.

'Now then.' The old farmer gave his usual greeting. Ben, his champion sheepdog, came out wagging his tail. John saw only Hannah standing there. 'Come in,' he said.

Hastily he reached for extra logs for the fire. 'It's a

bit nippy today. Let's get this door shut and keep the warmth in.'

He wasn't careful enough as he lifted the heavy logs. The tall pile shifted. Logs began to roll. Hannah looked up to see one toppling towards her. It would fall straight on to the little hedgehog.

Quick as a flash she twisted sideways and caught the log like a rugby player in both arms. It thudded against her chest, then she rolled to the ground with it. The hedgehog didn't move a muscle.

For a moment there was silence. John Fox looked down at the lucky creature. 'That was a near miss,' he whistled. Ben and Speckle came to sniff.

Hannah stood up. She brushed pieces of bark from her jacket. 'We think it's Spike.' She explained to John the story of the wandering hedgehog.

They wouldn't know for sure until he decided to unroll of his own accord. So the farmer ordered the dogs inside and set a small saucer down by the log-pile. 'Dog-food. Hedgehogs love it,' he assured them.

And sure enough, the smell drifted across. Down went the spines, out came the black, pointed nose and pale, furry face. The hedgehog marched to the

dish and waded straight in. Soon he was up to his middle in Ben's juicy dinner.

'Spike!' The twins beamed. They knew him at once.

'Daft little thing!' John Fox shook his head. 'Why isn't he tucked up nice and warm for the winter like all the rest?'

Helen and Hannah sighed. It was high time for this hedgehog to hibernate.

Three

Days went by and the weather grew still colder. A white layer of frost lay over Doveton Fell from morning till night.

Word went round school for everyone to be on the lookout for a little hedgehog, young and silly, who seemed not to know that it was time to sleep. Spike was seen one evening snorting his way through a rubbish bin outside Luke Martin's shop, then he was spotted next day recklessly crossing the road by Mr Winter's house. A car had to brake, the schoolteacher said. But then he'd lost sight of Spike in the hedge opposite. Everyone recognised him by his cheeky walk and his white face.

'The trouble is, he's young and daft,' Luke told the twins. 'A hedgehog has to get through is first winter before he learns any common sense.'

They'd gone into the shop with its colourful rows of tins, packets and jars, to hear about Spike's latest close shave. Laura Saunders had found him in her garden at the Manor and was telling Luke what had happened.

'It was lucky I was there. I saw him from my bedroom window, zigzagging across the patio towards the garden pond.'

Helen held her breath. Hannah whispered, 'Oh no!'

'Yes. He trundled along, right to the edge.'

'Was he after your dad's fish?' Helen pictured the big golden carp swimming among the reeds and pond weed.

Laura nodded. 'He didn't even stop to think. He just kept on walking straight into the pond with a big plop. I had to dash down to rescue him. There he was, his little face poking out of the water, doing the doggy-paddle for all he was worth.'

'They can swim?' Luke said, surprised.

''Course.' His nephew, Sam, had been listening from the back room.

'But he couldn't climb out. The sides of the pond were too steep.' Laura finished the tale. 'I had to run and fetch a pair of gardening gloves. I put them on and scooped him out of the water.'

'What did he do then?' Hannah gave a sigh of relief.

'Trotted off again, leaving a trail of wet footprints.' Laura laughed.

'Which way did he go?' At this rate Spike was using up all the nine lives he would have had if he'd been a cat.

'Down the drive, then I lost sight of him. But I

reckon he's had enough of village life, what with cars and garden ponds.'

The twins nodded and set off for home. It was after school, and Sam Lawson was heading their way too. They ran up the lane together, schoolbags bumping on their backs, a cold wind cutting through their padded jackets.

'I knew he couldn't look after himself properly,' Hannah said, worrying all over again about Spike.

'If only we could find out where he went.' Helen looked in the long grass to left and right.

'He could be anywhere,' Sam said scornfully.

His voice made the twins angry. He sounded as if it was stupid to worry about one little hedgehog. They were ten-a-penny, no one cared. So the twins stopped outside the gate to Crackpot Farm.

'Don't you like hedgehogs?' Helen challenged him.

Sam shrugged. 'I dunno. I never tried them.'

'Ha-ha, very funny.'

'We don't mean to eat.' Hannah outstared the fair-haired boy. 'They have enough to worry about without us humans putting them on the menu.' She began a list of dangers on her fingers. 'Badgers, dogs, magpies—'

'Slug-pellets, rat-traps, cars,' Helen continued.

'Drainpipes, bonfires—'

'OK, OK.' Sam stopped them. 'Look, if I see him round here, I'll let you know.'

They stopped in mid-sentence and stared. Sam Lawson had actually said something helpful. 'You will?' Hannah checked.

He nodded. 'Anyway, I need to catch a hedgehog for that science project,' he reminded them. 'We're supposed to study their habits or something.'

Hannah had already written her section on hedgehog habits. 'They like to wander,' she reminded him. 'You're not allowed to put them in a cage.' She didn't trust Sam; she wasn't sure why.

'Who says?' He turned his head away and scuffed the ground with his boot.

'The book says.'

'Oh.' He shrugged this off too. 'The book!'

Helen tugged at Hannah's sleeve. 'Come on!' It was no use trying to get through to him.

'You don't want to take notice of everything you read in a book.' Sam was cocky, because he thought the twins were town kids. What did they know about looking after animals, compared with proper farm kids? 'I knew someone who had a hedgehog as a pet. They kept him for years and years, fed him on bread and milk—'

'You're not supposed to give them milk!' Hannah refused to be pulled away from this argument. She *cared* about this.

'Who says? Yeah, yeah, the Book!' Sam set off laughing, up his track towards the farm.

Speechless now, the twins stared at his back. Knowing they were looking, he shoved his hands in his pockets and began to kick a stone, dribbling it as he went.

Hannah turned to Helen. 'Yuck!'

Helen nodded. 'Come on.'

They walked on up the hill, glad to see Speckle waiting for them at their gate, and the hens pecking in the yard. 'Let's hope Spike has the sense not to choose Crackpot Farm for the winter,' Hannah said quietly.

'When he could come to Home Farm instead,' Helen agreed.

'With good food.' Hannah reminded herself of the reasons why Spike should make his way up to them.

'It's warm and safe.'

'Nobody to bother him.'

'Freedom to come and go.'

This was a five-star hotel for a hedgehog, if he could only know it, compared to a prison if Sam Lawson got hold of him. Hannah knew that living in a cage would break Spike's adventurous heart.

'Sam wouldn't.' Helen dumped her schoolbag in the yard and stood looking down the hill. Yellow lights shone in the windows of Crackpot Farm. 'Would he?'

Four

In late November the skies clouded over and the frost eased.

'Good worm weather,' David Moore reminded the twins.

He was out with his camera one Saturday evening, hoping for a good photograph of the fox that had been seen right in the centre of Doveton village the night before. Helen and Hannah liked to go with him, to look and learn.

They'd chosen a spot opposite Luke's shop, since the fox was bound to be interested in his beautiful white doves which lived in a dovecote beside the house. They hoped the fox would creep through the dusk, yellow eyes gleaming, red coat glowing. The white tip of his tail would swish, the doves would call out a warning.

'And good worm weather means good hedgehog weather.' David Moore knew they would wake up to feed, even if their winter nests were already built. 'So keep a lookout for young Spike.'

There was no need to remind the twins that since his swim in the Saunders' pond, there had been no sign of the young wanderer.

They were busy with the fox, who came sure enough, prowling across the back yards of the cottages on Main Street. Doors were shut, curtains drawn. All of Doveton was safe indoors.

Hannah was the first to see the fox – his sharp snout and shining eyes. She pointed. Her dad aimed the camera. He took one, two, three good pictures.

Then, 'Shoo!' Up the street a door banged. 'Go on, get away, you little pest!' A dog yapped. The doves across the road fluttered inside their white wooden house. The fox had vanished into the darkness.

'Who was that?' David Moore wondered what the fuss could be about.

'It sounded like Mr Winter,' Helen said.

'And Puppy,' Hannah added. The dog's high bark pierced the silence.

'What's wrong with him?' Their dad couldn't take any more pictures of the fox. Instead they set off to investigate the noise.

In Mr Winter's long garden they saw the cairn terrier growling and worrying at what looked like an empty plant-pot by the garden shed. He made so much noise that Mr Winter had to come out of the house again.

'Puppy, be quiet!' the stern voice ordered. Mr Winter was a tall old man with a neat grey moustache. He liked everything to be in order. When he spotted the Moores by his gate, he explained that the dog was keeping watch over a hedgehog that had invaded his garden.

'Vermin,' he began, shaking his head. Puppy's bark had changed to a long, low growl. He guarded the garden shed while his owner talked. 'Nothing but pests, covered in fleas and goodness knows what!'

'What are?' Mr Moore tried to make sense of what was going on. The twins pricked up their ears. They were ready to stick up for Spike if necessary.

'Hedgehogs,' Mr Winter said again in a voice that was a gruff bark. 'Dirty little creatures spreading diseases.'

'No, they're not!' Hannah sprang to their defence.

Mr Winter simply ignored her. 'And cheeky too. Why, I just found one in my front porch, climbing into my wellington boot. Imagine, I might have put my foot on it!'

Yes, and it would have served you right, Helen thought. She gave Hannah a look that showed they were thinking the same thing. Mr Winter was bad-tempered about all animals except Puppy.

'Did Puppy see him off?' David Moore glanced at the growling terrier, tail up, trying to burrow under the shed.

'He certainly did,' the old schoolteacher said proudly. 'He chased him under there, it seems. Now the stupid little thing must be trapped.'

'Hedgehogs aren't stupid, they're—' Hannah began again.

Helen quickly drew her to one side. 'Shh! I think he must be talking about Spike!'

Hannah swallowed hard.

'Well, who else? He's the only hedgehog still tramping around, remember. Listen, Hannah, we've got to think!'

How could they get Spike out of another tight corner?

Mr Winter strode away towards the shed. 'What is it, Puppy? Is he making himself at home?' Without stopping to look, he took hold of a broom which was propped nearby. Then he began to poke and jab under the shed with it.

'Tell him to stop!' Hannah whispered to her dad, terrified that the long handle would whack Spike for six.

'Wait!' Helen opened the gate and ran up the garden. 'I've got a better idea.'

Mr Winter stopped jabbing and stiffly stood up straight.

'Food!' she cried. 'He'll come out if you give him something to eat.'

'Then what?' Mr Winter wanted to be well and truly rid of the hedgehog.

Helen thought quickly. 'Don't worry, we'll tempt him out of your garden for you.'

'Where to?' He didn't want the pest to keep on coming back.

'Down the street . . . a long way away . . .' She looked up and down for the answer. 'I know, we'll get him to head for the cricket field.' It was just down the road from here, at the edge of the village. It was an ideal, out-of-the-way place for a hedgehog. In winter no one would disturb him there.

By this time, David Moore and Hannah had joined them. 'I'll happily pay you for a tin of Puppy's dog-food,' their dad offered. 'That way we can get the little chap to follow us, no problem.'

Mr Winter ummed and aahed. At last he agreed that

the twins could carry out the plan.

So the schoolteacher and his rowdy dog watched from the window as Helen and Hannah knelt by the garden shed and let the delicious scent of dog-food float under it. Soon there was a snuffling sound, then a grunt. Then a furry fawn face appeared.

'Spike!' Hannah said softly. It was him, of course.

'Surprise!' Helen smiled. 'Yum-yum!' She coaxed him out of his hiding-place. As they backed off down the garden path, Spike's nose twitched. He followed like a pet lamb.

'Well done!' Mr Moore held the gate open. The twins backed out carefully. But Spike ran at the step to catch up with his supper. He tripped, rolled and fell on to the pavement.

'Oops!' Helen waited for him to pick himself up.

'Come on, Spike, this way!'

Patiently they lured him up the street away from Mr Winter's neat garden.

'Twins to the rescue!' Their dad led the way to the cricket field. 'One man, two girls, one tin of dog-food and one hedgehog!' He noticed the curtains twitch as the neighbours peered out. He laughed and took a photo of the odd procession.

But they made it in the end. Spike followed his nose yet again. Food, glorious food!

Five

'One fat and happy little hedgehog!' Mary Moore was pleased with the twins as she gave them their breakfast next morning.

'Yes, but two not-so-fat, not-so-happy girls,' David Moore pointed out. He enjoyed his Sunday breakfasts of bacon, eggs and toast.

'Why's that?' She noticed that Helen and Hannah had left food on their plates.

'We're worried,' Helen confessed. She'd snuck pieces of her bacon to an eager Speckle, who'd gobbled it down.

'About Spike,' Hannah added.

'Still?' Their mum couldn't see why. 'I thought you'd found him a nice safe place to stay.' She thought the cricket field had been a brilliant idea.

'Yes, but will he settle there?' Hannah wondered. True, they'd watched him scurry across the grass in the moonlight, but then they'd lost sight of him. And he was such a wanderer. How could they be sure he was safe?

'Maybe, maybe not.' Their mum could understand how they felt. 'You're worse than a couple of broody old hens,' she teased.

'Why not go down and check?' David Moore suggested. 'After you've washed up.'

Chairs scraped on the floor, dishes flew into the sink. The twins had washed up and were ready to go before he had time to turn round.

'And take Speckle with you,' their mum called, as they shot out of the house.

'Hello there. Have you two come to lend a hand?' Luke Martin was at the cricket field before them. He and Sam Lawson were clearing the pavilion for the winter. Sam frowned when he saw the twins and went inside.

'Hi, Luke. No, actually we didn't know you'd be here.' Helen stopped on the bottom step. For some reason she didn't want to say why they were here. 'We were just – er – passing.'

'Well, make yourselves useful now you're here,' he said cheerfully. He handed them brushes and dustpans. 'Help Sam tidy up inside, while I fix the shutters on the outside.'

'OK.' Hannah realised that finding Spike would have to wait. She told Speckle to sit, then went ahead into the dark pavilion. 'Hi, Sam.'

'Huh.' He gave more of a grunt than a reply. He was shoving benches across the floor.

The twins got to work with their brushes. Dust rose as their feet clomped over the floorboards. Hannah swept under the benches, Helen took mats to the door and shook them.

'Hey!' Sam coughed as the dust blew back in his face. He spat out bits of dried grass. 'Watch it!'

'Sorry.' Helen kept a straight face. Sam Lawson was always complaining.

He stared angrily. 'I'd like to know what you're doing here anyway.'

'Helping,' Helen said sweetly. She picked

up her brush and carried on.

When the pavilion was clean and tidy, Luke thanked them and got ready to lock up. 'Thanks a lot. Now everything's ready for next cricket season, so roll on spring!' He organised the village team and spent all his spare time looking after the pitch. The smooth wicket was his pride and joy.

Helen and Hannah went to join Speckle outside, while Sam sloped off by himself. They watched Luke stroll out to the middle of the flat field.

When he came back, he was frowning. 'That's funny.'

'What is?'

'There are a couple of holes there that weren't there before. Something's been having a go at the wicket – probably moles.' He shrugged and went off looking thoughtful. 'I'll have to do something about that,' he muttered.

'Uh-oh,' Helen said softly. She had a feeling that the damage wasn't caused by moles.

Hannah crossed the field to look. She found two small patches of bare earth in the smooth grass. Something had been digging with sharp little claws.

'Spike?' Helen asked her when she came back.

'Could be. The wicket's a good place for worms.'

They began to scout around for further clues. 'Let's hope he finally decided to settle down,' Hannah murmured, 'before he gets into any more trouble.' Luke wouldn't take kindly to having his cricket pitch ruined.

For a while they concentrated hard on their search. They looked for the little tramp by the walls, under trees, and finally back by the pavilion.

'What about under here?' Helen got down on all fours. The grass was wet and cold against her face, there was a strong musty smell from the dark, bare space under the pavilion. Beside her, Speckle was having a hearty sniff.

'Can you see anything?' Hannah joined her. 'No, Speckle, there's a good boy!' She pushed him away as he tried to lick her face.

'Can you see that heap of stuff over there?' Hannah strained to see. 'I think it's leaves. No, it's not! Yes, it is! Over there, Hannah, I think it's Spike's new nest!'

Hannah saw it too: a rough pyramid of dry leaves, twigs and moss, just like the one Spike had collected in their barn at Home Farm. Then she saw a movement, and the familiar shape of a young hedgehog slowly making his way through the shadows. 'Watch this!' she breathed.

Spike ambled up and dropped another mouthful of leaves on to the pile. He was so busy that he didn't notice they were watching. This was it – his real winter nest. The pile was high enough, the place was safe and dry. No noisy dogs, nobody coming and going. On odd days, when the weather was warm enough, he would be able to creep out and dig up that nice patch of smooth grass for worms.

Hannah and Helen swore they heard him give a happy sigh before he dived into his heap of leaves and began to turn on the spot.

Round and round, gathering leaves and twigs on his spikes. Round again, one layer after another, making a thick blanket all around himself. Soon they couldn't see hedgehog, only a spinning ball of leaves the size of a football. Then this, too, stopped moving. It settled against a pile of bricks which held up one corner of the pavilion, and lay there quite still.

Once more, Helen and Hannah could have sworn they heard a snore.

'Amazing!' Helen sighed. Her legs ached from

crouching, her back was stiff, but she was glad she'd seen this.

'Safe at last!' Hannah gazed at the still nest. No more foraging for food and wandering into danger. Spike, their wild hedgehog, had settled down for the winter.

'That's what you think,' a voice said.

They stared up at a pair of jeans, a thick blue jacket, a head with straw-coloured hair.

'Sam!' Hannah and Helen jumped to their feet.

'I *knew* you were up to something!' He stood, hands on hips. 'It's that hedgehog, isn't it?'

They were too surprised to deny it.

'That's what I thought when I saw you crawling about in the grass. So I went off to fetch Uncle Luke.'

'What did you tell him?' Helen's eyes sparkled with anger. What had Sam Lawson gone and done?

'I told him it was a hedgehog that made those holes in his cricket pitch.' He stared at them. 'Well, it was. And if it stays here, it'll make some more. I said it was making a nest under his pavilion!'

'Oh!' Hannah was speechless.

'So?' Helen challenged. 'What are you going to do about it?'

The twins stood in Sam's way, and Speckle began to growl.

He took one step back, then stood firm. There was a grin on his broad face. Behind him, coming through the gate carrying something large and square, came the figure of Luke Martin.

'Wouldn't you like to know?' Sam Lawson said. 'I'll tell you this for nothing, though. You won't like it, and there isn't a single thing you can do about it, so there!'

Six

'I'm sorry, Hannah, sorry, Helen.' Luke put the box on the ground. ' I know you mean well, but this just isn't the place for a hedgehog.'

'But he's built his nest,' Hannah pleaded. She prayed that Luke would change his mind. 'We can't disturb him now.'

'He has to sleep somewhere.' Helen backed her up. Luke was soft-hearted, and he was a friend. Surely he wouldn't turf a poor little hedgehog out into the cold, wide world.

Sam Lawson stood by. He leaned against the pavilion, hands in pockets, smirking.

Luke glanced at their worried faces, then shook his head. 'No, sorry, girls. He has to go!' He thought of his lovely, smooth cricket pitch and Spike's sharp little claws.

Sam stood up straight. 'Shall I grab him and put him in the box?'

Helen and Hannah blocked his way. Speckle sat beside them, ears pricked, waiting for orders.

'No, hang on just a second. We have to go about this properly.' Luke was thinking as he went inside the pavilion. 'We need something to pick him up with. Sam, come in here and help me look.'

The twins glared at the enemy as he followed his uncle inside. 'What are we going to do now?' Helen whispered.

Hannah gulped. She began to panic. 'We can't just let them grab him! You're not supposed to pick hedgehogs up unless they're sick. He might never be able to find his own way around again.'

'If they ever let him out of that horrible box!' Helen pointed at it. Luke must have brought it from his shop. It had BAKED BEANS written on the sides. She gave it a little kick of disgust.

Speckle jerked his head to one side. He looked at

the empty box. Helen gave it another sharp shove with her foot. Speckle bounded towards it. This was a good game; better than the usual one of fetching sticks. He sank his teeth into the soft cardboard and dragged the box along the ground.

Suddenly Helen's eyes lit up. Luke and Sam were still rummaging inside the pavilion. She looked at Hannah without saying a word.

Hannah read her mind and nodded. Speckle had given them an idea. He tugged and shook the box this way and that. He was a good sheepdog, ready to take and fetch whenever the twins gave him an order. So Hannah gave a low whistle. 'Away from me!' she called softly. It was the shepherd's command for his dog to set off up the hill with his group of sheep. 'Go on, Speckle. Away from me!'

Speckle took hold of the box between his teeth. He followed the order and dragged it away across the field. It bumped and bashed the ground. When Luke and Sam came out of the pavilion, their hedgehog box was fifty metres away, battered and flattened by the eager dog.

Helen and Hannah stood there, wide-eyed and innocent. Now Luke would have nothing to carry

Spike away in, all thanks to Speckle.

The shopkeeper held a fat leather glove in one hand. He frowned at the dog and the ruined box. They would have to think again.

'Maybe it's just as well,' Hannah said. 'Spike has a right to be here, after all.'

'What about my wicket?' Luke pictured a trail of destruction: leaves, scuff-marks, holes and bumps. It was too much to bear. He slid his hand into the wicket-keeper's glove, ready to go ahead anyway. 'I'm afraid it's your hedgehog against my whole cricket season,' he told them. 'Box or no box, he still has to go!'

Sam stamped down the wooden steps after his uncle. He took off his blue jacket. 'Wrap it in this,' he suggested.

There was no help for it. Spike was about to lose his winter home.

So the twins had to stand and watch as Luke lay down and wriggled under the pavilion. They couldn't see, but they heard him grunt as he inched closer towards Spike's nest. His head and arms had already vanished, only his legs stuck out. Sam crouched behind him, his jacket at the ready.

'Got him!' Luke's muffled voice cried. There was a
rustle of leaves, a little, high-pitched squeal.

Helen and Hannah closed their eyes tight. They
hadn't been able to save Spike, they had let the poor
little hedgehog down.

'Luke didn't even warn Spike what he was going to
do!' The twins had raced home with Speckle. Now
they poured out the full story to their mother.

'He just grabbed him in the horrible leather cricket-
glove! How would *he* like it?' Helen still had the sound
of Spike's squeal in her ears.

'I'm sure Luke must have thought it was for the best.' Mary Moore was sewing new curtains for the café. She sat in the kitchen, busy at her machine. 'He wouldn't be cruel on purpose.' She'd heard how they'd wrapped Spike inside Sam's jacket. 'They didn't hurt him, did they?'

Hannah was almost in tears. 'No. But, Mum, guess where they took him!'

'To Luke's?' She cut her thread and eased the flowery fabric away from the machine. 'He'll take good care of him, don't worry.'

'No, not to Luke's. That wouldn't be so bad. But Sam took him to his house! That was the worst thing about it,' Helen explained. 'Sam persuaded Luke to let him take Spike to Crackpot Farm!'

Mary paused. 'Ah, that's what's upsetting you.'

'He lied. He told Luke he had to do a school project on hedgehogs.'

'But he didn't say Miss Wesley told us never to try and catch a hedgehog in order to study it.' Helen remembered how clear their teacher had been. 'Do not on any account disturb a hedgehog,' she'd insisted. 'They're wild animals, and not to be touched. Your project must rely on watching them from a safe distance, and on books. Remember, no touching!'

'But Luke believed him. He said if Sam had to do a project, he could take Spike home with him.' Hannah recalled the boy's gloating face as he finally got his own way.

'And now he's a prisoner!' Helen slumped into a chair. 'He's caged up in some horrible box.'

Their mother sighed, turned her fabric and began to sew again. The machine hummed. 'Yes, it does sound horrible,' she agreed.

'He'll pine away,' Hannah said. 'He'll fade away and die!'

'Don't be so gloomy.' Mary Moore sewed steadily. She sounded thoughtful over the whirr of the machine. 'But I wonder what Sam Lawson can be thinking of, I must admit. Surely he doesn't mean Spike any harm?' She pictured him as a shy boy, but not vicious. His parents, Carrie and Neil Lawson, were perfectly friendly.

The twins were dead set against Sam. 'He's horrid,' Helen moaned, sinking further into her chair.

'He never listens.' Hannah told her mum how they'd warned him not to keep Spike in a cage. 'He just goes ahead and does things because he wants to.

He doesn't think of anybody else.'

She didn't know if it helped to blame Sam, but at least it took her mind off poor Spike, bundled up, jostled and bumped up the hill to Crackpot Farm, tipped into a bare, cold box with just a dish of milk and a lump of stale bread.

Seven

Luckily for the twins there was lots to do. This would be their first Christmas at Home Farm, their first Doveton school play, the first time they'd hung lights and decorated the farm kitchen with holly. And it was their first sight of snow on the top of Doveton Fell.

Then there were the animals. Each morning before school they went to feed them; hay for Solo in his stall, grain for the chickens roosting in the barn. Lucy the grey goose came cackling across the yard, Sugar and Spice sat snuffling at their wire door, waiting for breakfast oats.

Helen and Hannah woke early to do their chores,

then changed for school. There was hardly time to stop and think. School meant another whirl of activity, squeezing in lessons between rehearsals for their Christmas play. Hannah was in the choir and Helen helped backstage. Soon parents would come to see their version of *The Wizard of Oz*.

'Sam Lawson's the Scarecrow,' Hannah told her dad. She pulled a sour face.

'Because he hasn't got a brain,' Helen added. They still hated him more than anything.

After rehearsal it was already dark, so their mum or dad would pick them up from school and drive them home.

'Don't look so glum,' David Moore said, as he met them one afternoon. Kids streamed out into the playground and parents waited in their cars to collect them.

Helen got in and slammed the door shut. 'You'll never guess what.'

They waited while Hannah waved goodbye to a friend, then got in the other side.

'No, I won't,' he said, cheerful as ever. Helen in a bad mood was a sight to behold. She scrunched her lips into a tight button-shape and knotted her brows.

'She's been given a part in the play!' Hannah crowed. 'Natalie Green had to drop out, so Helen's the Lion!'

Mr Moore grinned. 'Better than a Munchkin at any rate.' He thought of the gang of little folk who lived in the world of Oz.

'No, it's not,' Helen snapped. She glowered out of the window. 'It means I have to be on-stage all the time with the Scarecrow.'

'Sam Lawson,' Hannah reminded him. 'She'll have to *talk* to him!' Half of her thought it was funny, half of her was relieved that she wasn't in Helen's shoes. Since Sam had taken Spike prisoner, neither of them had said a single word to the horrible boy.

'I have to go to an extra rehearsal with just him tomorrow morning.' It would be Saturday. The girls had planned to go riding with Laura Saunders. Now Helen would have to let Hannah go alone.

'That's tough.' David Moore started the car and drove off. As luck would have it, they followed the Land Rover from Crackpot Farm down the main street. They could see the dreaded Sam perched beside his mum in the passenger seat. When they were halfway up the lane, the Land Rover stopped and Carrie Lawson leaned out.

Their dad put his foot on the brake and wound down his window to listen.

'Tell Helen I'll give her a lift down to rehearsal tomorrow morning,' Carrie called. She was a normal mum – youngish, prettyish, with light brown wavy hair. Always busy and friendly, she wasn't the monster you'd expect from the way Sam Lawson had turned out.

'Great, thanks.' David Moore accepted quickly and arranged a time. The Land Rover turned off to Crackpot Farm, while they carried on up the hill. 'She's expecting you at their house at ten,' he told Helen.

'Thanks, Dad!' This was the end of a perfect day. 'First I'm forced to prance about on-stage with Sam Lawson. Then I have to miss riding. Now I have to get a lift in horrible his car!'

Their dad pulled up at Home Farm. 'There's no such phrase as "horrible his",' he said calmly, trying to hide a smile.

'There is now!' Helen flounced out of the car and went skidding across the icy yard. She ended up flat on her back, face to face with a surprised Lucy. 'Don't you dare laugh!' she warned the goose. This just wasn't funny.

'The Lion?' her mum murmured, when she heard the news. 'We must book our tickets. I shall look forward to this!'

Crackpot Farm stood at the end of a long, rough lane. It was an old house with a huddle of barns and outhouses, all built from the local Lakeland stone.

Helen went up to the door and knocked. She was surprised that it felt cosy and welcoming, with its bright green door, its shiny knocker, and a row of boots inside the porch. She'd been expecting to hate the house as much as she hated Sam Lawson.

Carrie and Sam were ready, so they climbed straight into the Land Rover. Squashed in between them, Helen spent the journey staring straight ahead until at last they reached the school.

'I'll meet you here at twelve,' Carrie Lawson promised as she waved them goodbye. 'Good luck with the rehearsal, Helen.'

She smiled. 'Thanks for the lift.' It was hard to stay in a bad mood when someone was so nice. Sam had walked on ahead.

'Don't mind Sam,' his mum said. 'He's shy, especially with girls.' She watched him disappear through the door. 'He's used to being by himself a lot at home on the farm. He doesn't find it easy to make friends.'

Helen was puzzled. This didn't fit with her picture of him. 'Thanks,' she said again as she turned and followed him into school.

Miss Wesley soon arrived and they worked hard all morning at their lines for the play. Helen had to learn to roar like a lion.

'That's very good!' Miss Wesley beamed, as Helen opened her mouth wide. 'But don't do it right in Sam's ear. You'll turn the poor boy deaf!'

Helen muttered sorry without meaning it. The next time she roared, she did it twice as loud, twice as near.

'Watch it!' Sam put his hands over her ears. Miss Wesley had been too busy at the piano to notice. He soon got his own back by flinging one arm across her face when Helen had to rearrange the Scarecrow's stuffing.

By the end of the rehearsal, the score was five-all – five deafening roars to five whacks from Sam's scarecrow arms.

'Well done,' the teacher told them. 'You'll make a very good Lion, Helen. I suppose that fits, since you're so fond of animals.'

They packed up and went out into the playground. 'I'll see you both on Monday,' Miss Wesley said. 'Learn your lines, both of you. There's less than a week to go.'

After she'd gone they stood awkwardly, looking this way and that for Carrie Lawson. There was no sign of the Land Rover.

'Don't you want to know how the hedgehog is?' Sam said suddenly. The words seemed to tumble out of his mouth without him meaning to say them.

Helen spun round. 'He's OK, isn't he?' Each night before she went to sleep, she lay thinking about Spike.

''Course he's OK.' Sam sounded offhand again. But now he'd brought up the subject, he had to go on. 'I made him a hutch.'

'What out of?'

'An old milk crate. One of those plastic ones. I took all the sections out of the middle and turned it upside down.' He stamped from foot to foot on the cold ground.

'Where did you put it?'

'On a shelf in the woodshed.'

'Does he like it?'

''Course.'

This was the longest conversation she'd had with Sam Lawson. She remembered his mum saying how shy he was and noticed that he was blushing to the roots of his fair hair. Oh well, at least he seemed to be taking care of Spike. 'Has he made a nest?'

'Sort of. I put torn-up newspaper and stuff inside his hutch.' Sam looked at her sideways. 'Do you want to come and see him?'

'Could do, I suppose.' She sounded casual, but really her heart had given a sudden thump. She could hardly wait to see Spike again. Just wait till she got home and told Hannah!

'OK, then.' He spotted the Land Rover. 'Come on.'

And so Helen took the lift and went up to Crackpot Farm with them. Sam's mum was happy that he seemed to have made friends at last. 'I kept telling him to go up and visit you girls all last summer,' she told Helen. 'But you know what boys are like. It was all cricket and athletics with him then. And in winter it's all football. Oh, and of course this pet hedgehog he wants to show you.' Mrs Lawson obviously hadn't heard the whole story of how Sam came to have Spike. 'He spends a lot of time looking after him.'

Slowly Helen began to change her mind about Sam Lawson. You could do the wrong thing for the right reason, she decided. Sure, it had been bad to turf Spike out of his nest, but Sam did care after all. Eagerly she followed him outside for a peep at the hibernating hedgehog.

'Shh!' Sam opened the shed door and pointed to a

blue plastic crate. It stood upside-down on a shelf on the wall opposite. Daylight came in through a small, cobwebby window. The air was chilly and damp. From inside the crate she could hear a faint scratching and scraping.

'Is he awake?' Helen asked, suddenly worried. It was nearly Christmas, time for all hedgehogs to be asleep.

'Yes. He doesn't need to hibernate. I give him lots to eat to keep him happy. Look.' He let her take a peek through the narrow slits in the side of the crate.

She saw a pile of torn newspaper, an empty dish . . . and Spike. Only, at first she wasn't sure it was him. Where Spike had been fat, this little hedgehog was thin. Where Spike had been happy trundling through the frosty grass, this one scratched miserably at the smooth plastic sides of his cage. 'Oh!' Helen let out a small cry. 'He wants to get out!'

'That doesn't mean anything,' Sam assured her. He picked up a silver tin from the shelf and opened the lid. 'Watch this.'

She peered over his shoulder as Sam dipped a large spoon into the tin. He drew out a heap of wriggling, white grubs. They twisted and curled on the spoon. 'What are they?' she gasped.

'Maggots. I buy them from the fishing tackle shop in Nesfield. Spike loves them.' He waited until the hedgehog had gone to scratch in a far corner of the crate, then quickly he lifted one edge. He tipped the maggots into the dish, then rattled it with the spoon. Spike's head went up and he sniffed. 'See!' Sam lowered the crate and waited for Spike to come and get his lunch.

But Spike, it seemed, wasn't hungry. He shuffled over to the wriggling pile, sniffed once and turned away.

'I thought you said he loved them?' Helen stared at Sam.

He shrugged. 'He does usually. Maybe he doesn't feel like food.'

'But Spike *always* feels like food!' She felt she had to whisper in this dark shed.

'Maybe he doesn't eat as much in the winter.'

'Or when he's been put in a cage!' Her hopes of finding Spike well cared for had faded. She looked inside the crate again; he was definitely thinner, slower, more unhappy.

'Now look,' Sam objected. If she was going to start moaning, she could go and take a running jump. 'If we'd left him in the cricket field like you wanted, something would soon have come along and grabbed him!'

'Something like what, for instance?' she hissed back at him.

'Something like that fox in the village. Or a badger. It was a useless place for him to build a nest. Anyone could've told you that!'

'Says you!' She was furious now.

'Yes, says me! Have you seen what happens when a badger gets hold of a hedgehog? I'll tell you. You go along the morning after, and all you see is a few prickles!'

Helen's hands flew to her ears. 'Stop it!'

'It's true. They get eaten. That's what would have happened to your precious Spike if we'd left him where he was!'

He stormed out of the shed and Helen followed. 'Look, I don't care what you think of me. Whatever you say, that hedgehog's only alive because I brought him up here.' He raised his voice and slammed the shed door. Helen stared at him in stunned surprise. 'If it wasn't for me, he'd be dead as a door-nail!'

Eight

'That's right,' Luke agreed. He was weighing jelly-babies for two brothers from Main Street. The sweets rattled from the scoop into a shiny metal dish. 'That was one of the reasons I agreed to move Spike. The cricket pavilion was a lousy place for him to spend the winter. It wouldn't have been five minutes before something had come along and snaffled him!'

Helen and Hannah had refused to believe it until now. Helen had raced home to tell Hannah what Sam had said. She'd found her in the barn, grooming Solo after her morning ride.

'*He* doesn't know anything about hedgehogs!'

73

Hannah had said scornfully. 'Sam Lawson thinks you should give them bread and milk!'

'He's feeding Spike maggots, and he hates them,' Helen had gabbled. 'He says Spike would be dead by now if it wasn't for him, but it looks like he's going to be dead before too long anyway. You should see him, Hannah. He's thin as anything. He hates being cooped up in that crate!'

'He should be free,' Hannah had agreed.

But what could they do? They brushed and combed Solo and led him into his stall. Then they went to find Speckle. The only thing for it, they decided, was to go into Doveton to plead with Luke.

But now he was agreeing with his nephew. 'You might not like it, but Sam did the only thing we could to save that little hedgehog from a badger or a fox! Have you any idea how many young ones die during their first winter?' He tipped the sweets into a paper bag and handed them to Billy and Harry Upton.

Hannah waited for them to pay their money and leave. She thought hard about what Luke had said. When the shop was quiet again, she began. 'We thought Sam wanted to take Spike away and keep him because of us.'

Helen nodded. 'Because he didn't like us.'

'What made you think that?' Luke always had time to listen. He leaned his elbows on the counter.

'He never wanted to talk to us.' Hannah remembered his silences, and how he turned away whenever they went near.

'And we thought he might be doing it out of spite,' Hannah explained. 'He knew we were worried about Spike, so he just sort of stepped him and took him away because he thought he knew best.'

'Hmm.'

The bell on the shop-door tinkled. Another customer came in. But Helen was too busy telling Luke how thin and ill Spike looked to stand aside. 'Sam keeps on saying he's fine, but I know Spike doesn't want to stay in that cage, Luke! He won't even make a proper nest, and he won't eat.' She pleaded with him to persuade Sam to let him go. 'Can't you talk to him?'

'And tell him what?'

'That hedgehogs have to be free.'

Luke sighed and stood up straight. 'I don't know that I can.' He shook his head. 'What do you think, Fred?'

The twins turned to look at the newcomer. It was the old farmer from High Hartwell, their other neighbour on Doveton Fell. He ran a dairy herd. He was a big man who plodded across his fields and never hurried. His broad face was crinkled and creased by the wind, sun and rain, his tweed jacket was the colour of winter heather.

'Think about what, Luke?' he rumbled, tipping his cap from his forehead.

'Do you think you can keep a hedgehog in a cage?'

Helen and Hannah hung on with baited breath for his reply. Fred Hunt was the sort who knew all the answers. He'd been born and brought up at High Hartwell. There wasn't a thing he didn't know about animals, both farm and wild.

'Well now, let's see.' He scratched his forehead. 'If you come across one that's been injured, that's when you have to pick him up and pop him in a cage. Just until he's better, mind. You can put a dab of disinfectant on the cut, or you can clip him free from whatever he might have got tangled around his legs. Then you have to keep an eye on him for a day or two until the leg's better. You keep him warm and give him plenty to drink.'

His slow voice rumbled on. Helen and Hannah could picture the farmer's huge hands gently untangling a hedgehog's tiny legs from a bundle of knotted string, or bean netting.

'But,' he said with a slow shake of his head, 'no, I wouldn't keep a hedgehog in a cage any longer than need be. I'd want to get him back on his feed and on the road again as quick as ever I could.'

The twins nodded hard. It was what they'd said all along. What would Luke do now?

'They like their freedom,' Fred insisted. 'Just like you and me, Luke. They don't take to being shut up in a cage.'

'Hmm,' Luke said again, and frowned. 'I see what you mean.'

'Mind you, it sounds as if you've got a bit of a problem on your hands now.'

The twins looked from one to the other, like people in a crowd at a tennis match – this way, that way, waiting for a final verdict.

'Why's that, Fred?'

'It's the wrong time of year.'

'To let him go, you mean?'

'Aye. Not many worms about, the ground's too

hard. Not many slugs and beetles neither.'

'You reckon he'd starve if we let him go now?'

Hannah and Helen saw that there was no easy answer.

'There's a fair chance of that, yes. On the other hand, I don't reckon much to his chances if he stays put in this cage.'

'He'll pine away,' Helen whispered. 'Why can't it be as simple as just letting him go?'

'If Sam agreed,' Hannah sighed.

Fred hunt was sorry he couldn't be more use. He bought some postage stamps and a loaf of sliced bread, then went on his way. 'Let me know how you get on,' he told them.

What now? The twins looked at Luke, but he too shook his head. 'I only wish I knew.'

'Talk to Sam,' their dad said. He was putting their Christmas tree in a tub. The tree had roots, so he filled the tub with earth from the field at the back of the farm.

'Easier said than done.' Helen held the tree straight while he trod the soil firmly down. 'I just had a row with him earlier today.'

'What's the matter? Couldn't he learn his lines?'

'No, it was about Spike, not the play.'

'Well, whatever. The only way you're going to get anywhere is if you start talking again.'

They stood back. Now they would take the tree indoors and fetch the decorations from a box in the attic. Their mum had told them where to look.

It was a lovely job; the twins always liked to decorate the Christmas tree. But this year Hannah's heart wasn't in it as they wound the fairy lights through the branches and hung the silver balls. She couldn't help feeling that their dad's advice had been right from the start. If they'd talked to Sam Lawson in the first place, then between them they might have been able to solve Spike's problems.

And it was still true now. As Helen reached to put the fairy on the top of the tree, Hannah went to fetch her jacket and hat.

'Where are you off to?' Helen asked. One twin rarely went off without the other one.

'Crackpot Farm,' Hannah said, quiet but firm. She hoped that Helen wouldn't offer to come this time. She could manage to talk to Sam Lawson better by herself.

Helen looked put out. 'It won't do any good.'

But their dad stood by Hannah. 'No, I think she should do it, Helen.' He wished her luck.

'She'll need it,' Helen muttered, going off to their bedroom in a huff.

Hannah knew they'd need more than luck if they were going to do what was best for Spike.

She ran down the lane and turned off along the track to the Lawsons' farm. Sam's mother was carrying shopping from the Land Rover into the house. She seemed pleased to see Hannah. 'Sam's in the shed with that precious hedgehog!' she said with a wave and a smile.

So Hannah went where she'd pointed, to a small woodshed at the far side of the farmyard. The door was open. Inside, she could see Sam crouched down. He tapped the edge of a dish with a spoon, and peered between some old sacks full of what looked like logs. He called out Spike's name.

When he felt Hannah's shadow in the doorway, he looked up. 'What do you want?'

She steeled herself. 'I want to talk.'

He stood up slowly. 'What about?'

'Spike.'

'You'd better shut that door.'

Hannah did as she was told. It made the shed dark and spooky. There were corners cluttered with rusty tins and old machinery. She could see an upturned plastic crate on a shelf. 'Where is he?'

'I don't know, do I?' Sam gave an exasperated sigh.

A flutter of panic rose in her chest. 'Isn't he in there?' She peered inside the blue box, and saw that it was empty.

'Don't worry, I let him out on purpose. He's in here somewhere.' He squatted again and tapped at the dish.

Hannah saw that it was full of things that wriggled and squirmed. She backed off towards the door. 'What's that?'

'Maggots,' he grunted. 'You saw them earlier, remember!'

'Oh!' She realised his mistake. No wonder he'd been so rude. 'No, I'm Hannah. That was Helen.'

He shrugged. 'Anyhow, what do you want?'

She swallowed hard, then crouched to help him look for Spike. 'I came to say sorry.'

'You what?' Sam stopped peering into the dark, cluttered corners and turned to stare.

'I said, we're sorry. We thought you didn't care about Spike. Now we realise you do.' There – she'd got it off her chest.

''Course I care. I buy him maggots out of my own money, don't I?'

Hannah took another peek at the dish. 'He doesn't seem to like them much, does he?'

Sam's face flushed. He looked as if he was about to lose his temper. But instead he decided to admit it. 'Do you think I should try something else?'

'Dog-food.' Hannah told him it was Spike's favourite.

'I never thought of that.'

'Not many people would. I could go and bring some from Home Farm,' she suggested.

'Now?'

She nodded.

'You could phone. Helen could bring it.' This time his face turned red from shyness. 'It'd be quicker,' he explained.

'OK, and I can stay here to help you find Spike!' She ran to the house to phone home. A grumpy Helen agreed to bring the food. When she got back to the shed, Sam had already found Spike between the logs.

Spike The Tramp

He held him wrapped up inside a piece of old sacking. The hedgehog's fawn face peered out. He blinked at the daylight as Hannah opened the door.

'He still won't eat the maggots,' Sam said sadly. 'I don't know what's wrong with him, going off his food like this.'

Very slowly, very carefully, Hannah went forward to stroke the top of Spike's nose.

He squeaked, but he didn't roll up and hide his face. His dark eyes shone, his ears and nose twitched as a fresh breeze blew into the shed.

'He misses the hedges and ditches,' she whispered. 'Don't you, Spike? You just want to be back on the open road!'

Nine

'Don't say it!' Helen had run down to Crackpot Farm with a tin of Speckle's food as soon as Hannah had rung. Now she was busy scooping it into a clean dish. Inside his blue cage, Spike scuttled up and down.

They'd all said it: *Sorry, everyone. But most of all, sorry Spike!*

'If anyone else says sorry, I'll scream!'

'I am, though,' Sam said as they watched and waited.

Helen slipped the dish into the home-made hutch. The hedgehog's sharp claws stopped rattling up and down the length of his cage. He snuffled. They waited. *Slurp, slurp, chomp*! The unmistakable sounds of Spike tucking in. They heaved three sighs of relief.

'We're all sorry,' Helen said. 'But that's not going to make him fat again, is it?'

'No, but Speckle's food is!' Hannah peered through the slits. 'Look, he's climbed halfway into the dish!' She laughed as Spike waded into the food.

'Hedgehogs can eat twenty per cent of their own body weight in one night.' Helen came out with an Amazing Hedgehog Fact.

Sam whistled.

'And they can drink a third of a litre of water.' She'd been reading the book. After Hannah had set off for Crackpot Farm alone, Helen had sat miserably on her bed, reading all about hedgehogs. By the time Hannah had rung, she'd come up with a brilliant idea.

'What else do they eat? Sam could see Spike gobbling and hear him snorting. His appetite had come back, thanks to the twins.

'Pilchards,' Hannah said solemnly. 'I haven't tried them, but it says so—'

'In the Book!' he laughed.

'Digestive biscuits,' Helen added.

They shook their heads.

'Honest! It says so—'

'In the Book!' they all said at once.

'So what we have to do is to get him really nice and fat.' Hannah thought ahead. 'Fat enough to stand the cold and last the rest of the winter.'

Inside the hutch, Spike grunted as if he agreed. He slurped at the water that Sam had just brought for him.

'Then let him go?' He looked worried. 'Are you sure he'd be safe?'

'I know it's risky,' Hannah nodded. 'But—'

'He'll die if he stays here? He'll pine away?' Sam believed it at last.

'If only we could work out a way of looking after him without keeping him cooped up.' Hannah saw that he'd finished the food and water, and was already scrabbling at the sides of the hutch, squeaking to be let out.

Now was the time for Helen's brilliant idea. 'I think we can!' she told them.

'How?' Hannah and Sam asked together.

'We can build him a proper nest-box at Home Farm,' she began. 'One made of wood, with a special way in and out. We can put food beside it, and make sure none of the other animals can get near!'

'We can?' Sam shook his head as if he doubted it.

'Honest!' Helen's eyes gleamed. She nodded hard. 'I've read about it—'

'In the Book!'

'Now for something I made earlier!' Helen wasted no time. While Sam stayed at Crackpot Farm with Spike, the girls ran home. Helen showed Hannah a wooden box. It was about thirty centimetres square, good and strong. 'Well actually, I didn't make it. I found it in the attic.'

The box was one of Mary Moore's jumble-sale finds. No one knew what it had been made for, but their mum was sure that one day it would come in useful.

Hannah told Helen how they could make it into a nest-box for Spike. 'We need to make a lid with a little hole for a tunnel to lead into it. And we'll need air-holes in this top side here.' She'd worked it all out from the book.

'How about a piece of pipe for the entrance tunnel?' Hannah suggested. They took the box outside and began to rummage in the barn.

'Here's a bit,' Helen said at last. It was a length of narrow plastic drainpipe that their dad didn't need.

Solo stamped his hooves and snorted from inside his stall, while the twins made plans.

David Moore said he would help as soon as he'd finished work in his darkroom. He lent them his hammer and saw. Their mum found a piece of wood that would make a perfect lid.

'We want to get it finished by tomorrow morning,' Hannah explained. 'Sam's bringing Spike up here after breakfast.'

'He is, is he?' David Moore had come to show them how to use a jig-saw to cut a round hole in the wood. 'Does that mean that you three are talking now?'

Helen tutted, Hannah made a face. 'Da-ad!' they protested.

He grinned as he watched Helen slot the pipe into the hole. 'You'll need a sealant to cover the cracks.' He went about finding everything they needed to make the perfect nest-box.

'What do you think?' Hannah asked their mum as soon as the sealant was dry. 'Spike will be safe from badgers because they won't be able to squeeze down the tunnel. And he can fill it with leaves and grass, and

get fresh air through these airholes, see?' She was proud of their box. It was a luxury hotel for a hedgehog.

'It looks fine. But where will you put it?' Mary asked. They all went out into the farmyard to look for the best place.

'Somewhere safe,' Hannah said.

'Somewhere warm.' Helen knew that the box must be protected from the icy winter winds.

'Somewhere quiet.' Hannah sighed, as Speckle bounded into every corner, sniffing out interesting smells.

'That cuts out everywhere, then,' Helen said with a frown. She knew that they wouldn't stop Speckle from nosing around his own yard.

'Spike has to be able to find it easily, otherwise he won't use it.'

'Yes, but it has to be out of Speckle's way.'

They were stuck. The yard had plenty of friendly spots for a hedgehog; the roots of the chestnut tree, the compost heap, a hawthorn hedge by the far wall. But Speckle liked to play in all of these places.

'Got it!' David Moore had a brainwave. 'Wire netting! We make a fence around the nest-box. Spike can get through, but it keeps poor old Speckle out.' He gave the dog a pat as he went to fetch the giant roll from the barn. 'So where do you want to put the box?'

It was growing dark as finally they chose the most sheltered corner. There was an old stone trough beside the hedge, and a space in between just large enough for the box. The earth was soft here, so they dug down, lined the hole with polythene and settled the box into it, packing the earth tight around. Then they piled stones on top, and more earth, so that the entrance looked like a small cave.

'The soil will keep it nice and warm.' Hannah patted hard. She'd found moss to make the earth look better, and made sure that the airholes were still clear.

'We can plant bulbs and have flowers in the spring.' Helen was satisfied as she stood up and brushed the soil from her hands.

'Right, stand back!' David Moore unrolled the wire netting. He surrounded the hidden nest-box, while Speckle sat watching, head tilted, one ear cocked. When the netting was in place, fixed into the ground with wooden stakes, he went up to it and sniffed.

'Sorry, Speckle, no entrance!' Helen looked on.

Soon he gave up and went to chase dead leaves under the tree.

The twins had worked hard. They'd solved many problems, and now they were ready.

'Let's hope Spike likes it,' Hannah said later that night, as they lay in bed. The sky was starry, the air cold and crisp.

Tomorrow Sam would bring him to Home Farm. They would give him one last feed and show him his new home. After that they would set him free. They'd done all they could. The rest would be up to Spike.

Ten

Sam arrived at Home Farm next day as Helen and Hannah prepared a hedgehog feast in the kitchen.

'Pilchards for main course!'

'Digestive biscuits for dessert!'

The twins presented two dishes to Sam.

'It's Spike's Christmas dinner.' Hannah invited him into the yard to see the nest-box. 'Guess where?'

It was well hidden. 'Behind that new wire fence?'

She nodded and showed him the secret entrance, and explained that no other animal would be able to get in.

'Do you think he'll like it?' Helen asked. She was

more nervous than she admitted. 'We're going to put his dinner inside the fence. 'He's meant to smell it and scramble through.'

'We hope!' Hannah had had her fingers crossed all morning. 'And then we'll lay a trail of treats to the entrance. Spike is supposed to follow it. Then he'll creep inside and go to sleep after his dinner.'

Sam examined the arrangements and nodded. They went back inside without speaking. Spike sat on the table inside his blue hutch, little knowing what lay in store.

'Can I take him out to his nest-box?' Sam asked. His voice was breathless, though he hadn't been running. He wanted to be the one to set Spike free.

The twins nodded.

'You're the one he knows best,' Hannah whispered.

They gazed at little Spike as Sam slipped his hand inside his Uncle Luke's wicket-keeper's glove. He'd brought it along specially.

'Come on, Spike, I'm not going to hurt you.' He talked softly as he slid his hand under the hedgehog and lifted him out.

Spike blinked up at them. He was already putting

on weight, his eyes were bright. His pale, whiskered face seemed to grin.

'This is it, then.' Helen opened the door and led the way across the farmyard.

Hannah followed with the dishes of food and water, and then Sam, with Spike held close to his chest. He talked to him as they went, explaining as if Spike understood every word.

'Now, Spike, you're to eat up all your dinner. It's good for you. I'm going to put you inside this fence. Yum, smell those pilchards!' He cradled Spike in the glove as he lowered him to the ground. Gently he tipped him off. 'Go on, Spike, scrummy dinner!'

The hedgehog tumbled and rolled. He got to his feet with a snort. He turned his head this way and that, nose twitching. There were fresh-air smells coming at him from every direction. But the strongest and best was the smell of food. Down went his snout, snuffling towards the dishes. His little feet scampered across the stony ground. Then he was waist-deep in pilchards, slurping fish, smacking his lips and sighing.

'So far, so good,' Helen whispered. They were scared to disturb him as he ate.

The pilchards were soon gone. Now for the

biscuits. *Munch, munch* through the crumbled treat, until this dish too was empty.

'He'll burst!' Sam said, watching wide-eyed.

'Look at him drink!' Helen saw the water dish drain rapidly.

'Now!' Hannah relied on Spike's greed. There was a thin trail of biscuit crumbs into the nest-box.

Sure enough, Spike the Hoover got to work. The crumbs vanished into his mouth. He crept nearer and nearer to the home they'd built.

Sniffing and gobbling right up to the tunnel, Spike ate the last of the crumbs and peered down it. He scuffed at the loose earth, wriggled his backside, turned full circle. The twins and Sam couldn't bear to look.

Spike took one step inside, then another. He backed out to check his surroundings. For a moment their hearts sank. But he seemed to think he was safe. He tried again. This time his head and front legs vanished into the darkness. Then his hind legs. He was inside the box!

It was like climbing a long hill and getting to the top. It was like clouds lifting.

'You did it!' Mary Moore brought them all inside and gave them hot chocolate. 'Well done!'

'We'll keep an eye on him.' Hannah promised Sam. 'We'll see you at school tomorrow and tell you how he's getting on.'

'And now you'd better get back home and learn those lines,' David Moore reminded him. 'I promised your mum I'd take you down before lunch.'

But Helen had a better idea. 'Why not stay here?' she suggested, furious with herself for blushing red as a beetroot. 'We could learn our lines together.'

Hannah sneaked a grin at her mum, then straightened her face. 'What?!' she protested in a high voice when Helen glowered.

'Nothing! Just don't say anything!' she hissed, as Sam went to phone home.

'I never!' Hannah laughed out loud. 'I'm off out for a ride,' she told them, whistling as she went.

During the afternoon the sky clouded over, threatening to bring snow. Helen and Sam sat by the living-room window. They looked out from time to time. All was quiet by Spike's nest-box. They imagined the little hedgehog soundly snoring.

Mrs Moore was sewing in the kitchen and Mr Moore was working in the darkroom when Hannah rode back to Home Farm with Speckle in tow. Helen glanced out of the window at the sound of the pony's hooves in the yard. Sam flung down his book, stretched and yawned. He was fed up with Scarecrows and Lions. There was a football match on TV that had started half an hour earlier.

'I'm off home,' he told Helen. 'It's United versus Villa.' He paused by the door. 'You won't tell anyone, will you?'

'Tell them what?' There he was, going on about football, forgetting to say thanks.

'About you and me – um – rehearsing together.' He shuffled his feet. 'I don't want Harry Upton to know.'

Helen tossed her head. 'As if!'

They might have had another row, if Hannah hadn't come in looking worried. She'd left Solo standing in the yard, ready for grooming. His saddle was off and she was unfastening his bridle, when Speckle went nosing towards Spike's nest-box. She called him, then decided to go over and take a look.

'Did either of you tip Spike's dishes upside-down?'

she asked. 'Because I've just looked, and they're all the wrong way up.'

'No.' Helen had made sure that no one had gone near. She wanted to give their lodger chance to settle in.

'That's funny.' Sam didn't wait to hear any more. He went out to look for himself.

Helen followed. 'Maybe Spike did it? Maybe he wasn't asleep after all?' She knew that hedgehogs often overturned their dishes, looking for insects and millipedes hiding underneath.

'Do you think he's still hungry?' Hannah wished he wasn't so restless. She glanced up at the darkening sky.

'Who knows? Maybe he's gone back in for a snooze,' Sam said to himself more than anyone else. He listened hard for sounds of the little creature snoring.

But Hannah was alarmed. 'It's the wrong way round. He should be sleeping during the day, not wandering around out here.'

'We should have kept a better lookout.' Helen blamed herself.

'Well, never mind now.' Hannah felt the worry

clouds lower again. She watched the dry leaves scurry across the farmyard in the high wind. 'Maybe he came out to gather stuff for his nest.'

'To make himself cosy,' Sam agreed.

'To keep himself warm.' Helen hoped it was true. But she had a dreadful feeling that the box was empty.

It was Speckle who proved her right. They were saying goodbye to Sam at the gate, trying to pretend that everything would be OK, when the dog began to root amongst the leaves under the tall bare tree. They hardly noticed him, sniffing and wagging his tail as usual, until suddenly he gave a sharp yelp.

He sprang back from the pile of leaves, whining and whimpering. Hannah gasped and ran to him. There were specks of blood on his nose. She held tight to his collar and calmed him.

'Spike!' Who else? Hannah and Sam searched among the leaves. There he was, unrolling from his prickly ball. He trotted as fast as his legs could carry him . . . *away* from his nest-box.

He headed for the gate.

'What shall we do?' Sam watched him sprint. 'Should we cut him off?'

'It's no use.' Helen shook her head and held him

back. 'If Spike doesn't want to stay, there's no point trying to force him.' He'd dived under the gate out on to the lane. The tarmac on the road must have felt strange underfoot, so he scuttled into the ditch.

Helen glanced back to see Hannah taking Speckle inside. 'Let's go part of the way with him,' She said to Sam. They followed Spike into the lane.

'Can't we pick him up and take him back?' Sam begged. He had to run to keep up.

Helen felt light snowflakes fall on to her face. 'And then what? He'd turn round and run all over again.' She knew in her heart that he was born to wander.

'Look, there he is!' Sam spotted him rustling through the frosty grass, intent on setting out up the fell.

They both thought of him tucked up safely in his nest-box instead of heading out across the snowy hill. Something caught in Helen's throat; they'd tried so hard to give Spike a home.

But she could understand it, as she stood in the gently falling snow, watching him trundle off. 'He doesn't want a roof over his head,' she said sadly. 'We knew that right from the start.'

Sam heard. He stopped to watch Spike vanish into

the dusk. They lost sight of him in the long grass, saw him swerve out across the lane and disappear again. Helplessly they watched him on his way.

He went steadily now, settling into a rhythm, ready for the long haul to wherever it was he wanted to go.

Eleven

The Wizard of Oz was a success. Helen roared her way through her part as the Lion, Sam walked with scarecrow-stiff legs and outstretched arms, searching for a brain. Mums and dads clapped and sang 'Somewhere over the Rainbow' as the final curtain came down.

Mary Moore hummed the song as she drove the twins home after the last performance. They all sang along. It was a play about a girl with a dream.

The car bumped up the lane. The snow which had fallen the weekend before had soon melted. Now the ground was damp, soggy and dark in their headlight beams. As they turned into their yard, Hannah yelled out a warning.

'Mum, stop!'

There was a screech of brakes. There in the yellow beam was a small spiked ball. It was dead still, caught in the glare.

Mary More switched off the lights and engine. They sat in the dark and waited for the hedgehog to unroll. Could their own dream come true? Had Spike come back to make his nest at Home Farm after all?

Helen and Hannah clutched the front seats, peering over their mum and dad's shoulders through the front windscreen.

'It's him, I know it is!' All week Helen had been putting food down just in case. So far, the dishes had stood untouched.

'Don't get your hopes up too high,' their dad warned.

Mary sat silent, glad that she'd been able to stop in time.

Slowly, very slowly, the hedgehog judged that it was safe to emerge. His nose peeped out, then his short legs appeared.

'Is it?' Hannah hoped and prayed.

A face looked warily all around – the furry, alert face of a hedgehog who knows that danger lurks nearby.

'No,' David Moore said quietly. The face was too dark, the muzzle grey and grizzled. 'That's not Spike. 'That's just an old chap on a jaunt on a mild winter's night.'

Helen sighed. Hannah closed her eyes and sat back. 'Never mind.' Their mum waited for the old hedgehog to amble out of the way. He shambled off, plodding on to the grass verge, taking his time. At last she could ease the car through the gate.

No one spoke much. The twins went inside and straight to bed.

'You know the worst thing?' Hannah whispered from under her warm duvet. She stared up at the cracks in the ceiling, seeing animal shapes in every one.

'What?' Helen thought the worst thing was hoping for a few seconds that Spike had come home, then realising he hadn't.

'Not knowing where he is or if he's safe.' It wasn't the same as taking in a stray dog or an unwanted pony. You could look after them, and you always knew they'd be there to go home to. 'With Spike we'll never know if he's even alive!'

On the afternoon of Christmas Eve the weather was fine enough to ride Solo out on to the fell. Sam had taken to joining them on his mountain-bike whenever he saw them trekking across the hill. As usual, Speckle made up the party.

They chose a bridleway away from the farmland, up on to the wild moors. The wind tugged at them, but there was a bright sun. Looking back down into the valley, Doveton Lake shone; a long finger of silver water between two steep mountainsides.

Hannah urged the pony on ahead. They'd agreed to go as far as a tall, pointed rock known as The Needle. Then they would change round. Sam was to take a turn riding Solo. Now the going grew tougher. Low heather bushes straggled across the narrow track. She concentrated on guiding Solo safely through.

'Hannah, what's Speckle up to?' Helen yelled from below. She'd stopped pedalling and stood astride her bike. From this angle, all she could see was the flash of Speckle's white tail bobbing through the sea of heather, taking a short cut to The Needle.

'He's OK.' Hannah had a better view. He was bounding through the bushes on legs like springs. Then he vanished in the undergrowth.

'It wears me out just looking,' Sam said.

Helen kept on watching. There seemed to be a pattern in Speckle's actions. He would leap up the hill, bark once, then bound back down towards Hannah and Solo. But Hannah didn't take any notice, so he ran back up to The Needle, barked, turned and ran to her. 'I think he wants to show us something,' she said slowly.

Speckle sat looking up at her. His pink tongue lolled, his sides heaved in and out. He yapped, then turned to toil up the hill.

'Come on!' Sam dropped his bike and began to run across country. He wanted to reach the rock before Hannah and Solo. 'Let's go and see!'

Helen took up the challenge. But the heather tripped her and tugged at her feet. The hill was steep. It was slow going.

Speckle ran down to encourage them. This time he was more excited. He barked, ran a few steps, then barked again.

'Wait, Speckle!' Helen gasped. She and Sam

staggered the last few metres. They arrived just as Hannah approached by the bridleway.

'I didn't know it was a race,' she said, dismounting.

'It wasn't. Speckle wants to show us something.' Helen felt her lungs would burst. She noticed Sam double over to catch his breath. Then he dropped to his knees and began to crawl across the small clearing at the foot of the tall, thin rock. He followed Speckle on his hands and knees.

Hannah glanced at her sister. Had Sam gone mad?

Helen shrugged. Both Sam and Speckle stalked across the short grass. There was nothing for it but to follow. They left Solo standing quietly, and crouched down and crept after them.

Ten metres from the rock Speckle stopped. *Close enough*, he seemed to say. Once bitten, twice shy. Helen and Hannah joined Sam. Together they tried to make out what Speckle had seen.

'There!' Sam pointed.

The twins made out a telltale pile of leaves and twigs, mixed up with dry bracken, birds' feathers and moss. There was a trail trodden by small feet through the grass. It was hedgehog's nest waiting to be made. That was it; Speckle had picked up a scent and followed it here. He sat waiting to be praised.

'Good boy, Speckle! Hannah put an arm around him. 'Well done.'

'Hang on a minute, maybe this stuff has been here for ages.' Sam thought it could be a pile of nesting material left over from the autumn and not used.

Helen shook her head. 'No, the scent must be fresh for Speckle to pick it up.' This was a hedgehog who was late making his winter home.

'So where is he?' Hannah, usually the patient one, got up to take a closer look.

'No, wait!' Sam held on to her. 'I think I heard something!' He pointed to the far side of the clearing.

Slowly plodding out of the undergrowth, footsore and weary, came the little traveller. His mouth was full of leaves, he limped along. But nothing would stop him now. He'd found his perfect nesting place high above the farms, way out of human reach. Steady and slow, Spike crossed the clearing.

They said his name under their breaths: 'Spike!'

'Don't go any nearer,' Sam warned. 'You know what he's like. If he realises we're here, he'll shoot off.'

So they watched from a distance. By now Spike was

Jenny Oldfield

an expert nest builder, since this was at least his third. One in the barn at Home Farm, one under the cricket pavilion, and now one on Christmas Eve in the shelter of The Needle.

He studied his heap of leaves. He hadn't seen the three of them, so he trundled round to choose the best angle. Then he ran at the heap, dived in and sent twigs and moss scattering over the grass. He began to turn. Leaves caught on his spikes, layer after layer, until all they could see was a whirling rubbish-tip on legs. Then he rolled up into a final ball and rocked into position in a cranny in the rock, under a low bush. He was safe from passing badgers, foxes, dogs . . . and human beings.

They rode home in high excitement, pedalling, cantering, bounding through the heather. There was Home Farm down below, lights already glowing, smoke curling out of the chimney.

'Mum!' Hannah cried, racing into the kitchen. 'Everything's OK. We've just seen Spike!'

Mary Moore was cutting pastry circles for the mince-pies. Her face was flushed from the warmth of the oven, she had smudges of flour on her cheeks. 'That's

114

good,' she said softly. Then she carried on humming Dorothy's tune from *The Wizard of Oz*.

'Aren't you surprised?' Helen gasped. Her hair was wild and knotted from the scramble down the hill.

She looked up and smiled. 'Since we came to live at Home Farm, *nothing* surprises me.'

David Moore came in. He held a sprig of mistletoe over his wife's head and gave her a kiss. Helen, Hannah and even Sam dived behind the table for cover. Speckle barked.

Hannah popped up again. She braved the mistletoe kiss. 'Speckle found Spike. He picked up his scent.'

'Good for him.' Their dad hung the mistletoe over the doorway. He winked at Sam.

'Why isn't anybody surprised?' Helen demanded. She stood up, hands on hips. 'We've run all this way to tell you Spike's safe, and you act as if you knew all along.'

'Well . . .' he began.

But Mary Moore stepped in, wiping her hands on a tea towel. 'Wait a sec – you say you ran all this way to tell us? Where exactly did you find Spike?' she asked.

'On the moor!'

'By The Needle!'

'He finally found somewhere to build his nest.' Sam finished the story. He beamed from ear to ear. 'Way out in the middle of nowhere. He just tramped off as far as he could.'

'Are you sure?' Mary Moore looked from one to the other.

'Yes!' What was wrong here? Helen stared back.

'Why?' Hannah quizzed.

Their dad opened the door. 'Come with me.' He beckoned them into the yard, and led them to the stone trough where the home-made nest-box stood. 'Then who's this?' he whispered.

They looked and strained to listen.

'Someone's in there!' Sam thought he heard a snuffling and snorting.

Mary nodded. 'Shh. We saw him go in about half an hour ago.'

'We wanted it to be your surprise Christmas present,' their dad said. He drew a scroll of white paper from his pocket and opened it up. WELCOME HOME, SPIKE! it said in big red letters.

'But . . .' Helen shook her head. 'Dad, Spike's made his own place up the fell. We just saw him!'

'Then who is this?' His face fell. He let the paper roll up again.

'Look out, here he comes,' their mum warned.

They stepped back as feet shuffled along the pipe and a face appeared at the tiny tunnel entrance.

'That's not Spike!' Sam said straight off. This was a big old hedgehog, only just able to squeeze in and out. His body was fat, he trundled out to sniff the air. His dark eyes twinkled as he caught their scent.

'It's the old grey one from the other night.' Helen recognised the grizzled face.

'We nearly ran him over, remember!' Hannah smiled at the ambling, shambling old thing.

David Moore pointed to the empty dishes by the nest-box. 'You mean to say, I've given him Spike's Christmas dinner?' He had opened a new tin of dog-food specially.

Hannah giggled. 'It looks like it.' The hedgehog flipped a dish over. He nosed for grubs and worms.

'I bet he couldn't believe his luck,' their mum laughed. 'First-class lodgings, free food. No wonder he's come back for more!'

The hedgehog must have heard them laughing. He looked up and turned over another empty dish.

Nothing put him off his hunt for food.

'He's certainly the granddad of all hedgehogs!' David liked his cheek. 'I bet he's seen a good few winters already. He knows all the tricks.'

The more the twins saw of him, the more they liked their new guest. He had a lopsided walk, and one ear was chewed at the tip. Best of all, he wasn't shy.

In fact, he came right up to the wire netting and peered up at them. He studied the row of curious faces staring down at him. Then, when he'd looked for long enough and no food appeared, he grunted and turned away. He waddled straight back into the nest-box. His fat little body squeezed out of sight.

Hannah turned to her dad. 'Can I borrow a pen, please? She took the scroll of paper from his pocket and laid it flat. 'Hold this end, Sam. Helen, hold this!' She got to work on the big red letters.

They watched her cross out SPIKE. She wrote new letters over the top. Now the message read: WELCOME HOME, GRANDDAD!

'Can we adopt a granddad?' Helen wondered aloud. Sam helped Hannah to stick the notice on the wire fence.

Her mum and dad stood, arms round each other's

waists. 'It looks like *he* adopted *us*!' Dad said.

Inside his nest-box the hedgehog rustled his leaves into position and settled down. Spike the Tramp had chosen the life of the open road, and Granddad had chosen them.

The twins sighed happily. As far as Christmas presents went, as far as dreams over the rainbow stretched, they agreed that Granddad was the best thing anyone could ever possibly wish for.

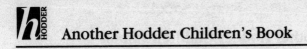

Another Hodder Children's Book

*If you've enjoyed this book, look out for the
other books in the Home Farm Twins series.*

SPECKLE THE STRAY
Jenny Oldfield

A lost puppy, trapped in a dangerous quarry!
Has he been abandoned there?

The twins long to keep him –
but what if the owner comes back?

If you've enjoyed this book, look out for the other books in the Home Farm Twins series.

SINBAD THE RUNAWAY
Jenny Oldfield

Sinbad needs a home while his owner is on holiday.

The twins adore the fluffy black cat, but he leaves a trail of chaos wherever he goes!

And then he runs away.

Can Helen and Hannah find him –
before he gets into real trouble?

If you've enjoyed this book, look out for the other books in the Home Farm Twins series.

SOLO THE HOMELESS
Jenny Oldfield

Solo's owner doesn't want him any more.

Helen and Hannah would love to have the pony – but their parents can't possibly afford to buy him.

Can Speckle, the twins' lovable dog, solve the problem?

HOME FARM TWINS

Published by Hodder Children's Books

66127 5	Speckle The Stray	£3.50	❑
66128 3	Sinbad The Runaway	£3.50	❑
66129 1	Solo The Homeless	£3.50	❑
66130 5	Susie The Orphan	£3.50	❑
66131 3	Spike The Tramp	£3.50	❑

All Hodder Children's books are available at your local bookshop or newsagent, or can be ordered direct from the publisher. Just tick the titles you want and fill in the form below. Prices and availability subject to change without notice.

Hodder Children's Books, Cash Sales Department, Bookpoint, 39 Milton Park, Abingdon, OXON, OX14 4TD, UK. If you have a credit card you may order by telephone – (01235) 831700.

Please enclose a cheque or postal order made payable to Bookpoint Ltd to the value of the cover price and allow the following for postage and packing:
UK & BFPO – £1.00 for the first book, 50p for the second book, and 30p for each additional book ordered up to a maximum charge of £3.00.
OVERSEAS & EIRE – £2.00 for the first book, £1.00 for the second book, and 50p for each additional book.

Name ....

Address ....

....

....

If you would prefer to pay by credit card, please complete:
Please debit my Visa/Access/Diner's Card/American Express (delete as applicable) card no:

Signature..

Expiry Date ....